The Berenstain Bears

ON TIME

Stan & Jan Berenstain

A GOLDEN BOOK · NEW YORK

Western Publishing Company, Inc., Racine, Wisconsin 53404

ISBN: 0-307-23173-9

6:59

It is almost seven,
as you can see.

All is quiet
in the Berenstain Bears'
Home Sweet Tree.

7:00

The cubs are asleep.

At seven o'clock

the alarm goes off.

It's quite a shock.

7:05

Five minutes later
they're back to sleep.
Both Brother and Sister
are still asleep!

7:10

Papa's coffee
starts to perk,
and Papa will soon
be heading for work.

7:15

And off to work
is Grizzly Gus,
the driver of
the cubs' school bus.

7:20

Gus's bus starts

on its way

to pick up cubs

for school today.

7:25

What about Brother
and Sister Bear?
Will they be ready
when Gus gets there?

7:30

The bus stops here.

The bus stops there.

It picks up bear

after bear after bear.

Will our cubs be ready?

It's quite a worry.

They may not be—

unless they hurry.

7:35

But are *they* worrying?

They are not.

Are they hurrying?

They are not.

If you checked,

you would find

sweet sleep is all

that's on their mind.

7:40

Gus picks up Bob
and Liz and Fred.
Can Brother and Sister
still be in bed?

7:45

Ma sees the bus.
She starts to worry.
To catch that bus
her cubs must hurry.

She has not heard
a single sound—
her cubs aren't even
up and around!

7:50

No more dreams
for Sister and Brother.
They wake up to
an angry mother.

7:55

That old school bus
is almost there—
at the house
of Brother and Sister Bear!

7:56

Hurry! Hurry!
Rush! Rush! Rush!

7:57

Wash and dress
and comb and brush!

7:58

Downstairs! Downstairs in a flash!

7:59

Eat some breakfast! Off you dash!

8:00

Down the steps
into the bus
and say hello
to Grizzly Gus!

Moral:

If you sleep past seven,

you might be late

when the school bus comes

for you at eight!